S0-BIH-061

This book belongs to

....

Peppa Pig™

LADYBIRD BOOKS

UK | USA | Canada | Ireland | Australia | India | New Zealand | South Africa

Ladybird Books is part of the Penguin Random House group of companies
whose addresses can be found at global.penguinrandomhouse.com.

www.penguin.co.uk   www.puffin.co.uk   www.ladybird.co.uk

Penguin
Random House
UK

First published 2019
001

This book copyright © Astley Baker Davies Ltd/Entertainment One UK Ltd 2019
Adapted by Lauren Holowaty

This book is based on the TV series Peppa Pig.
Peppa Pig is created by Neville Astley and Mark Baker.
Peppa Pig © Astley Baker Davies Ltd/Entertainment One UK Ltd 2003.
www.peppapig.com

Printed in China

A CIP catalogue record for this book is available from the British Library

ISBN: 978-0-241-40502-4

All correspondence to:
Ladybird Books
Penguin Random House Children's
80 Strand, London WC2R 0RL

MIX
Paper from
responsible sources
FSC® C018179
www.fsc.org

Peppa's Australian Underwater Adventure

WILLOUGHBY
JB
0 1 NOV 2019
CITY LIBRARY

Peppa was very excited. She had just won a Great Barrier Reef art competition at the aquarium.

"Congratulations, Peppa," said Miss Rabbit. "Your prize is to join me on a marine-biology trip to Australia!"

"Hooray!" cheered Peppa. "What's marine biology?"
"It's learning about the plants and animals that live
in the sea," explained Miss Rabbit.
"Ooooooh," said Peppa.

"We're going to stay with Mrs Kangaroo," continued Miss Rabbit. "She will teach us how to scuba-dive in the Great Barrier Reef." "What an amazing prize for a competition!" said Mummy Pig, a bit surprised.

"Well, Peppa's drawing was very imaginative," said Miss Rabbit. "Her picture wasn't exactly like any fish I have seen, but it was a prize-winning picture."

"I see," said Mummy Pig. "There's nothing wrong with a bit of imagination, is there?"

"Of course, you, Daddy Pig and George
will be coming to Australia, too," Miss Rabbit
told Mummy Pig.
"How lovely," replied Mummy Pig.
"Thank you, Miss Rabbit!"

Peppa and her family were **very** excited to be seeing their friends in Australia again.

"We'll be leaving first thing tomorrow," said Miss Rabbit. "Right, then," said Mummy Pig. "We'd better head to the shops and get everything we need for the trip."

Peppa, George, Mummy and Daddy Pig headed to Mr Fox's shop and told him what they needed. Mr Fox got everything out. "Now," he said, "I think you'll also need some paper and colouring pens. You never know when they might come in handy."

"I'm not sure we do –" began Mummy Pig. "Trust me, Mummy Pig," Mr Fox interrupted. "You definitely need these."
"Oh. OK, then," said Mummy Pig. "Thank you for your help, Mr Fox. We must get going now, so we can pack all of this!"

The next morning, Peppa and her family woke up **very** early
and hopped on the aeroplane to Australia.
"Where's Miss Rabbit?" asked Daddy Pig.
"I think she's finding her own way there," replied Mummy Pig.

While Peppa, George, Mummy and Daddy Pig flew on an aeroplane, Miss Rabbit travelled to Australia by . . .

hot-air balloon . . . Whoosh!

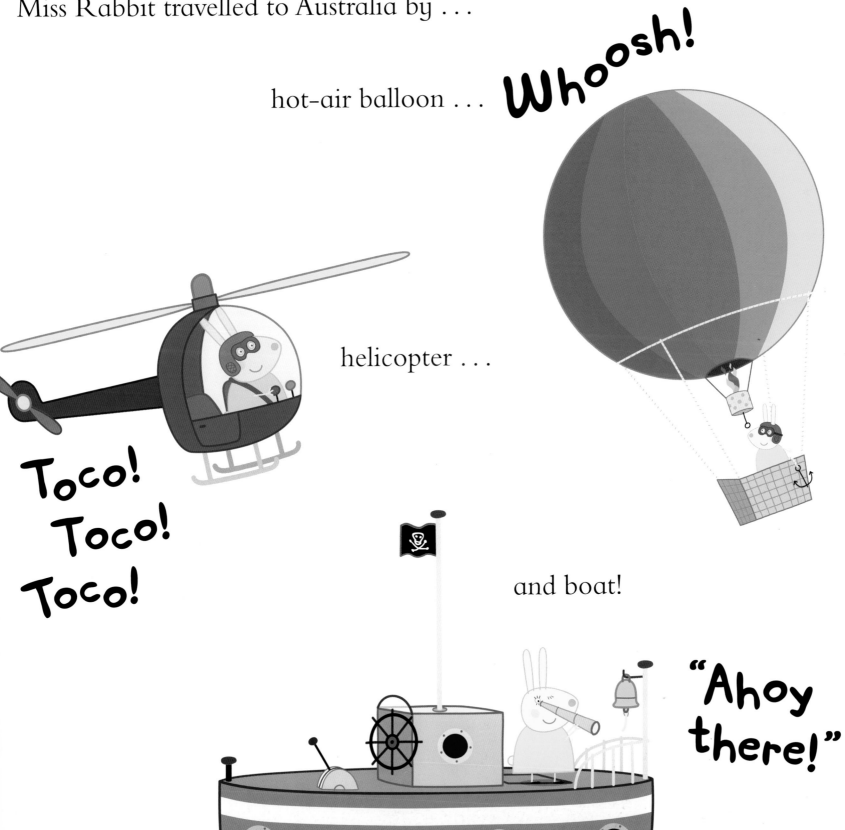

helicopter . . .

Toco!
Toco!
Toco!

and boat!

"Ahoy there!"

Amazingly, Miss Rabbit arrived in Australia at the exact
same time as Peppa and her family.
"Welcome to Australia, everyone," said Mrs Kangaroo.
"It's **SO** good to see you," said Kylie Kangaroo, giving Peppa a big hug.

After they were settled in, Mrs Kangaroo went through the diving plan with Kylie, Peppa and Miss Rabbit.

"There are so many amazing creatures to discover in the Great Barrier Reef," she explained. "It's an incredible place."

Mrs Kangaroo taught Peppa about diving and marine biology.
"What does 'buddy-up' mean?" asked Peppa.
"It means we are going to dive in a group," explained Mrs Kangaroo.
She held up a list of the creatures they were going to see and count
on their underwater adventure.

Green sea turtles . . .

orange
clownfish . . .

blue starfish . . .

pink sea
anemones . . .

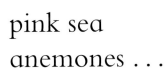

and even whales!

"Wow!" gasped Peppa.
She was so excited.

Mrs Kangaroo drove everyone to the boat.
Then they hopped on board with their
diving gear and headed out to the diving site.

SPLASH!

SPLASH!

SPLASH!

SPLASH!

When the boat stopped, Mrs Kangaroo gave Peppa and Kylie a special underwater list each. "It's important that we count the marine life carefully," she said. "If you spot anything unusual, let me know."

Then Peppa, Miss Rabbit, Kylie and Mrs Kangaroo jumped backwards off the boat. They dived **deep** down under the water to the reef.

The divers saw lots of amazing plants and animals on the reef. They spotted . . .

five orange clownfish . . .

four pink sea anemones . . .

three brilliant blue starfish . . .

two big green turtles . . .

and
one
enormous
whale!

"Wow!" said Peppa.
"It's so colourful down here."

Peppa and Miss Rabbit followed the whale further into the reef. Peppa used her diving fins to swim as fast as she could to keep up, and Miss Rabbit paddled along behind her.

The whale pointed its fin at a big rock.

Peppa peered behind the rock and saw a
fish that wasn't on Mrs Kangaroo's list,
poking its head out.

"That looks just like the fish I coloured in!" said Peppa.

At the end of the dive, everyone climbed back on board the boat.
"We counted SO many creatures!" cried Peppa excitedly.
"It was amazing! I also spotted a beautiful fish that wasn't
on your list, Mrs Kangaroo."

"What did it look like, Peppa?" asked Kylie.
"It looked a bit like the clownfish," said Peppa.
"But not exactly."
"Hmm," said Mrs Kangaroo, "can you
describe it a bit more, Peppa?"

Peppa used the colouring pens
from Mr Fox's shop to draw the
fish she had seen. It looked just like
her picture from the aquarium.
"Wow, that's a lovely fish, Peppa!"
said Kylie.
"Peppa is very good at drawing,"
said Miss Rabbit.

"I don't believe it!" gasped Mrs Kangaroo when she saw Peppa's drawing. "It looks just like a rare blue clownfish that hasn't been seen for a while now. Where did you spot it, Peppa?"

Peppa took everyone back to where she had seen the unusual fish. Mrs Kangaroo had been searching for the blue clownfish for a long time. Peppa spotted the whale winking at her in the distance. "Thank you for showing us the fish, lovely whale!" Peppa said, winking back.

After Mrs Kangaroo had taken lots of photographs of the fish, she signalled for everyone to swim up to the boat and head back to shore.

That afternoon, Mrs Kangaroo and her family cooked
a big meal to celebrate Peppa's amazing discovery.
"What do you think of the Great Barrier Reef, Peppa?"
asked Daddy Pig.
"It's the most brilliant place ever!" replied Peppa.
"The fish are just like I imagined they would be!"

Ho! Ho!
Ho!

She held up her picture from the art competition.
It looked exactly like the fish she had seen
on her dive.
Everyone laughed.

Hee!
Hee!

Peppa loves the beautiful Great Barrier Reef.
Everyone loves the beautiful Great Barrier Reef!